To the young man who has astonished us
and continues to surpass what
we were taught to expect and believe.

WaltonWorks
Belnor, MO 63121

Publisher: WaltonWorks, LLC
Editor: Linda Wolf, Network Publishing Partners, Inc.
Illustrator: Michael J. McBride, M&M Studio

Printed in the United States of America
First Edition: March 2021

ISBN Paperback: 978-0-578-86785-4

Library of Congress Control Number: 2021905413

About Kaleb

Tickle Me, Grandma is inspired by Kaleb, who has autism and is nearly nonverbal. These memories I'm sharing are from his early days. From the beginning of his life until today, he has been a jovial and playful person, always laughing and smiling broadly when spoken to. As a very young child, he would watch my facial expressions intensely. I could tell he wanted to interact and to communicate but couldn't put his thoughts and emotions into words.

One day, when he was about three, as he was smiling at me, I started to laugh and asked, "What do you want, little boy?" I began to tickle his tummy, and he burst into laughter with a joyous grin that lit up my heart. After that, when I saw him coming toward me with that grin on his face, I'd say, "Do you want Grandma to tickle you?" Soon, his new favorite phrase was "Tickle me, Grandma." It became our signal to begin play time—time to be free and enjoy laughing together.

When Kaleb began preschool, I would often pick him up afterward and discuss with his teachers how his day had gone. They'd speak of the daily activities accomplished and the new words they were working on with him, things he had experienced anew, and phrases that he'd spoken for the first time. The aide in his class told me how Kaleb was asking her as well as other teachers to tickle him by saying, "Tickle me, Grandma." They'd each explain who they were and that his grandma was not there. Eventually, his vocabulary expanded as well as his comprehension, and he found new ways to ask for chances to just have fun with people.

I will always remember those younger days, when he taught me as much as I taught him about how to get along in this life.

At night after a warm shower and a lot of splashing under the faucet, Kaleb bursts out laughing. It's his way of saying, "I'm done, Grandma!"

"Are you ready to come out and dry off?" Grandma calls from the next room.

No words are spoken as Kaleb climbs out of the tub.

He quickly reaches to turn off the water, then touches the towel to his chest.

Grandma is in the doorway now. "You have not dried your bottom or your legs," she points out.

Kaleb is busy watching himself in the mirror. He smiles, makes different faces, and jumps up and down to get a better view. Then he races into his bedroom, giggling.

“It’s time to dry your bottom and your legs,” says Grandma again. This time, she says it more firmly and more slowly. “Then put on your pajamas.”

She gives him a direct glare.

Kaleb stalls a little until Grandma starts moving toward him. Then he hurries to dry himself. He opens his drawer while announcing, "I need help."

"No, you don't," Grandma says calmly. "You are very… very… capable."

Completely frustrated, Kaleb begins to stomp and cry in his usual way of handling problems.

Grandma pulls him near and tickles his neck to calm him down. When she feels his heart slow down again, she heads for the kitchen. Kaleb hums as he pulls on his pajama pants.

Now, he is distracted by his tablet on the bench. The noise of cartoons begins to fill the room.

Then he hears Grandma coming back up the stairs.

Uh-oh! He grabs his top and frantically tries to put his arms in before she reaches the door.

“Kaleb, you know you should be getting in bed.”

He climbs in with the tablet in his hand and turns with a hopeful look at Grandma. She smiles and says, “Alright, just for a little longer.”

A calm comes over Kaleb while he rests with his tablet in bed. Sleep is slowly sneaking in. He struggles to stay awake, then smiles and giggles as he stirs under the sheet.

Keeping his eyes closed, he grins and says softly, "Tickle me, Grandma."

She leans toward him and reaches for his feet. Before she even touches him, Kaleb giggles nervously, then bursts out laughing. Grandma laughs, too.

She loves to watch his delightful reactions to the game they have played so many times. She tickles his ears, and then his feet as they laugh together. His laughter slowly quiets down and melts into a long yawn.

Grandma removes the tablet from his limp hands. “Did you say your prayers?” she asks.

His soft voice drifts through the dark room. “Thank you, Jesus, for my day, and I am healed, **AMEN!**”

That loud **AMEN** wakes him up a little. He yawns again and whispers, “Tickle me, Grandma.” But instead, she rubs his back until he totally relaxes and gives in to sleep.

In the morning, Kaleb awakes and comes downstairs, all dressed for the day.

"**Breakfast!**" he announces in a loud voice.

"Are you ready to eat?" Grandma asks, looking him over with approval.

"Yes." Kaleb's answer is *Yes* to almost every question. If he wants to say *No,* he is silent, with a smirk.

He digs into the hot cinnamon oatmeal with gusto and hums while he eats. Grandma urges him to finish up because it will be time to leave soon.

He puts his coat on and grabs his backpack to head for the door.

“Come with!” he says.

As Kaleb buckles up in the car, he watches everything that's going on outside. He's already thinking ahead to another great day at school.

CPSIA information can be obtained
at www.ICGtesting.com
Printed in the USA
LVHW071619120421
684239LV00004B/144